Late One Night

written by
Jan Mader

illustrated by
Jennifer McConnell

Late one night
I heard a noise.
It made me wide awake!

Late one night
I heard a noise.
It made me shake and shake!

Late one night
I heard a noise.
It made me cover my head!

Late one night
I heard a noise.
It made me scared to speak!

Late one night
I heard a noise.
It made me tiptoe from my bed!

Late one night
I heard a noise.
It made me hide behind the door!

Late one night
I heard a noise.
It made me sneak a peek!

Boy, can my dad snore!